What Goes UP

by
Pa...

tiger tales

Once, at the bottom of a big hill,
sat a dragon named Martin.

And Martin was sad.

The children in the village loved Martin very much.
"What's wrong?" they asked.
Martin flapped his tiny wings. He longed to fly,
but his wings were just too small.

"What goes up, must come down," he sighed.

Just then, a bumblebee
buzzed by in his yellow
and black jacket.

"Stripes must be the key to flying!"
Martin cried.
So he painted himself some stripes,

and leaped high into the air. . . .

But . . . CRASH!

"What goes up, must come down," said Martin.
He couldn't fly with the bees.

Then Martin watched the autumn leaves
blowing from the trees and he thought,

"Maybe if I sat in a tree,

I could fly away with the leaves."

He climbed up into
a tree and waited,

and waited,

and waited . . .

until the last leaf had blown away, leaving Martin sadly behind.

He couldn't fly
with the leaves.

So he lay on his back and watched the clouds flying in the sky and he thought,

"I must make myself as fluffy as a cloud. Then I could fly!"

Martin rolled in
white dandelion fluff

until he looked
just like a cloud.

Then he ran and took
a leap into the sky . . .

and he could fly!

For a moment anyway.

Tumble . . . tumble . . . CRASH!

"What goes up, must come down," said Martin.

He

felt

so

low.

Just as he was about to give up, the children
had one last idea.

"Don't worry, Martin!" they
said. "We'll show you how to
fly. You just have to believe."

Together they ran and flapped their wings.

They imagined the ground far below
and the birds and clouds all around them.

Day after day, they played their game
and flapped their wings some more.

And with all the exercise, Martin's wings began to
grow stronger and bigger . . . and he hadn't even noticed.

Martin felt

on top

of the

world!

But,
"Look out,
Martin!"
cried the children.

Over he went!

Martin whizzed down the hill,

scooted through town,

and sped past shops. . . .

FASTER and FASTER

the tricycle took him.

Martin couldn't stop.

He was out of control!

Until . . .

whoosh!

The road disappeared, and so did Martin,
right into the sky.

And what goes up,

must come down.

But Martin believed and he spread his big, beautiful wings, and to his surprise he found that . . .